ALL ACTION

MOUNTAIN BIKING

BOB ALLEN

LERNER PUBLICATIONS COMPANY
MINNEAPOLIS

Titles in this series
Backpacking
Canoeing
Climbing
Mountain Biking
Skiing
Skateboarding
Survival Skills
Wind and Surf

All photographs are reproduced by permission of Bob Allen except for *back cover* (Michele Dieterich), pp. 4, 11 (Geoff Parr), 22 (Mountin' Excitement), 31, 43 *right* (Eye Ubiquitous).

Front cover: A mountain biker on the run in California

First published in the United States in 1992
by Lerner Publications Company

Copyright © 1991 Wayland (Publishers) Limited
First published in 1991 by Wayland (Publishers) Ltd.
61 Western Rd., Hove, East Sussex BN3 1JD England

Library of Congress Cataloging-in-Publication Data

Allen, Bob, 1961-
    Mountain biking / Bob Allen
        p.   cm. — (All action)
    Includes index.
    Summary: Describes the development of the sport of mountain biking, its equipment, riding techniques, and competitions, and profiles some outstanding racers.
    ISBN 0-8225-2476-7
    1. All terrain cycling — Juvenile literature.   [1. All terrain cycling.]   I. Title   II. Series.
GV1056.A45   1991
796.6—dc20   91-17109
                                        CIP
                                        AC

ISBN 0-8225-2477-5

Printed in Italy
Bound in the United States of America
1 2 3 4 5 6 7 8 9 10 00 99 98 97 96 95 94 93 92 91

Contents

BEGINNINGS

From crowded city streets to isolated mountain peaks, mountain bikes are everywhere. You cannot open a cycling magazine or walk into a bike shop without the color and excitement of the sport grabbing your attention. Mountain biking has captured the imagination of a whole generation of riders. For all ages of kids and adults, this sport can offer fun in the sun (or the mud, or the snow) to anyone who gives it a try.

Not so long ago, there was no such thing as a mountain bike. Although the idea of riding off the road has been around since the first bicycle, it took some overgrown kids from northern California to spark the excitement that created the first mountain bike. What started as a single downhill race among a few friends in Marin County has become one of the world's fastest growing and most popular sports.

The riders who gathered for the first downhill dash wore jeans and heavy shirts and rode old bicycles that used **coaster brakes.** They called the trail they rode "Repack," because it was so steep that the riders used their brakes all the way down. When the bearing grease in their brakes burned up, the racers had to repack their brakes with new grease. They had no rules about what the bikes should look like, but these downhill pioneers preferred heavy old Schwinn frames. You might not recognize one as an ancestor of the modern mountain bike!

The first mountain bikers quickly found out that the heavy-duty parts and frames they needed did not exist. So they went on to build some of the first mountain bikes. Many of these riders are still building bikes and bringing new ideas and products to mountain biking.

The outcome is a style of bike and of riding that has captured the imagination of a whole generation of adventurers. The speed and excitement of cycling on the road are combined with the freedom to go where you want, across some of the roughest terrain in the world. You can grind up a slope, take it to the limit on a descent, or do a **slalom** through a forest. Whichever you choose, you will find that the spirit of adventure that started mountain

Gary Fisher was one of the downhill pioneers who raced the Repack in Marin County, California. His old Schwinn was one of the first clunkers —heavy bikes put together from bits and pieces. Some of Fisher's ideas helped to form the modern mountain bike, and through his design and manufacturing company he is still at the forefront of the mountain biking world.

The perfect getaway vehicle for a mail carrier—the dog just can't keep up

biking is still at the heart of the sport.

Having total confidence in your ability (and realizing that you are only limited by your imagination) is necessary to any sport. To ride a bike down a radical descent, ski down a mountainside, or surf in monster waves, you have to believe you can do it. If you are not sure of yourself, you could easily fail.

Why do mountain bikers take up the sport? There are probably as many reasons as there are riders. Champion racer Deb Murrell got into mountain biking because of a dream.

"All I wanted was a horse when I was young, but I couldn't have one. I started riding a road bike in the hills pretending it was a horse. I would tear up and down the bridle paths doing things which that bike wasn't capable of surviving. I didn't think about it, I just did it. I'd get covered in mud and love it. The great thing was just being outside."

RIGHT

Deb Murrell is one of the best riders in the United Kingdom.

World Champion John Tomac gained much of his superior handling skill from riding BMX (bicycle moto-cross). "I started out in BMX at four years old and was racing by seven. I practiced every day." Every time Tomac races, he is using the skills he developed when he was riding in his backyard at a very young age.

From the moment you took your first steps, you were starting to learn how to ride a bike. Climbing trees,

LEFT

The thrill of a fast ride through a forest

running, and jumping all develop the balance and coordination used in mountain biking. Even if you have never ridden a bike before, other experiences help develop your natural ability and become a base for your mountain biking skills. Any cycling you have done will be useful when you start riding off-road.

It is not the bike but the attitude you have when you ride it that counts. You could ride a BMX or an old road bike. But these will not perform as well as a specialized mountain bike. Mountain biking is about going out with a bunch of friends, racing around neighborhood trails, getting dirty, and having fun. Mountain bikes have broken the restraints of the road and made the biking world an endless adventure. So get out there and ride!

MACHINERY

ABOVE

This rider put nails through his tires to grip the road.

LEFT

A suspension system for mountain bikes

can get confused. But if you buy a bike made by a company that specializes in mountain bikes, you will be sure to get a bike that will do the job properly.

Having a flashy bike might impress your friends, but your riding skills are what really count. You will not have more fun because you spent more money. Sometimes you can get inexpensive, second-hand bikes. Check out the newspaper's classified ads or the bulletin board at your local bike shop to see what is available. But do not buy a second-hand bike without carefully checking it for problems. An experienced mechanic should look at the bike before you part with any money. Some bikes need only minor adjustments. Others have hidden damage.

Once you decide that you are going to buy a mountain bike, do not just buy the first one you try. Look at as many bikes as you can to see what is available. Find out which one is best for you and your budget. Most of all, do not be confused by advertising hype. There are so many sizes, shapes, and components to choose from, even experienced riders

The most important consideration when buying a bike is that it is the right size. When standing over the top tube of the bike, you should have at least two inches (five centimeters) clearance between the tube and your crotch. Do not let someone sell you a bike that is too big by claiming you will grow into it. Riding a bike that is

A young rider on
a bike with a
dropped top tube,
designed for
smaller people

too big is very dangerous. When you are in traffic or on the trail, you need to be able to steady yourself by putting a foot on the ground.

Many cycle companies build mountain bikes for small people. These have either small wheels or a top tube that slopes down, or both. A bike with a sloping top tube and full-size wheels is more easily modified to fit you as you grow.

It seems as though almost everyone is wearing flashy, tight-fitting cycling clothes. These are a good way for manufacturers to make money, but you do not really need them to go mountain biking. Baggy shorts and T-shirts, or sweat pants and sweat shirts, are fine for riding.

Because of the hazards of riding off-road or in traffic, a helmet is a good investment for safety. Wearing glasses or goggles can protect your eyes from sand, mud, and overhanging branches. And if you know that you will be riding over especially rough ground, you should also wear knee and elbow pads.

If you start to ride often, there are some clothes you might want to invest in to make riding more comfortable. Cycling shorts with seamless padding in the crotch will add comfort on a long ride. A pair of padded cycling gloves may prevent your hands from getting sore. Whatever you buy, make sure you buy it because you need it, not because everyone else has got one. Mountain biking is about how you ride, not what you wear.

TECHNIQUE

Good riding style comes from riding often. Experience builds on experience, and soon you will be performing moves that you never thought possible. All it takes is practice and a desire to improve.

Start by getting a feel for how the bike stops. When riding a bike for the first time, practice braking at slow speeds. Apply the brakes together, with slow, steady pressure. The front brake of a mountain bike usually has more power than the back brake, and it must be used with care. There is no better way to fly over your handlebar than to quickly pull on the front brake alone.

The brake levers should be positioned so that when you brake completely, the levers stop about an inch (2 or 3 cm) from the handlebar. Your braking grip also needs to be as comfortable as possible from the start. Many riders hold the bar with two fingers and the levers with two. Then they can brake quickly without losing their grip over rough ground. Experiment to find out what

hand position works best for you.

Before taking the bike off-road, also practice quick, sharp stops. Really squeeze on the brakes and feel how your weight is thrown forward. To avoid accidents, you will need to anticipate the braking action and move your weight back while bracing yourself with your arms. When descending, you should lightly

When buying a bike, you often pay more for less. The top-line mountain bikes are very light. To build these featherweight machines, the builder uses materials such as titanium, aluminium, and carbon fiber to shave off the weight. These high-tech components and materials are expensive and add to the cost of a bike.

FAR LEFT and ABOVE

While descending, put your weight at the back of the bike for better control.

squeeze and release the brakes so that the wheels do not lock. This action is called **feathering.** Also remember that you need a lot more space to stop in if your tire rims are wet.

Accurate shifting and good pedaling technique are critical skills for off-road riding. The time lost by a missed shift can lose a race for even the most experienced pro. And it could mean that you have to get off and push the bike up the hill.

The gears and rear derailleur. Try to remember which gear you are in without looking down.

Keep up a constant pedaling speed over different types of terrain. Try a speed of between 60 and 80 revolutions a minute, or more than one spin a second. You might feel a little silly pedaling this fast, but you will develop a smooth **cadence** that makes cycling easier. Change the gears as necessary to keep pedaling at a steady speed. To ride faster, select the next higher gear and try to maintain your spin. Pushing too hard wears you out and can damage your knees. Speed and strength come from a good, steady spin.

Mountain bikes have either 15, 18, or 21 speeds. As on a 10-speed bike, you will want to be in a low gear for extra power and in a high gear for going fast. But the shifters on a mountain bike are mounted to the handlebar where you can easily reach them with your thumbs.

The shifters mounted on the handlebar control the **derailleurs** that change gears. The front derailleur is controlled by the left shifter and moves the chain between different-sized **chainrings** on the **crankset.** The rear derailleur (the right shifter) moves the chain across the cogs on the **freewheel.**

Avoid the extremes of gearing. The combination of either the big chainring to the large freewheel cog or the smallest chainring to the small cog in the back causes chain and tooth damage, which is expensive to

fix. Try to remember what gear you are in without looking down. If you do not watch the trail, you could end up sitting in the dirt!

Most shifting systems are not designed to be used under hard pedal pressure. So when you are climbing, you need to let off the pressure just long enough to shift gears. This does not mean you should stop pedaling! Just ease off a little. If the chain rattles after shifting, move the shift lever slightly until the rattling stops. You will soon learn how to recognize noises and how to adjust the gears so that the sounds will disappear.

CLIMBING

Climbing is an integral part of the sport, because riding in the hills is what mountain biking is all about. To become a good climber, learn how to shift your weight to control the way the tires grip the ground. Out-of-the-saddle pedaling will give you power on short, sharp climbs. On a long climb, stay in the seat or you will quickly get tired.

For all kinds of climbing, move your weight forward. You can do this by bending your arms to bring your upper body over the front of the bike and sitting forward in the saddle. The combination of arm bending and saddle sliding will improve your climbing. Moving too far forward, though, will reduce the rear wheel's grip and let it spin. Practice will teach you how you and your bike climb best.

"Gear down going into the climb and keep spinning as it gets steeper," advises UK mountain bike champion Tim Davies. "Look ahead and anticipate what gears you'll need."

When the going gets tough, you may find yourself walking with the bike. Pushing it is fine if the trail is smooth, but if it is rough and rocky you might have to carry it. It is best to carry the bike over your right shoulder so the oily chain stays away from

LEFT

Out of-the-saddle climbing is best for short, fast bursts.

RIGHT

You might even have to carry the bike if the hill is steep.

"When I first started climbing, the front wheel would bounce off the ground and I'd fall off the back of the bike. I learned that by moving my weight forward I could maintain the right balance on the bike and control this unwanted (and painful!) wheelie."
Sally Hibberd, top racer

your clothes. Reach through the frame with your right arm and lift the bike so the top tube rests on your shoulder. Steady the handlebar with your left hand. Wrapping a pad around the top tube makes carrying your bike much more comfortable.

DOWNHILLING

After a long, hard climb, you have certainly earned the downhill to follow! Downhills are probably the most exciting aspect of mountain biking. They can also be the most dangerous. Because it is easy to accelerate out of control, do not speed down an unfamiliar trail. You never know what could lie ahead to throw you off your bike.

As the trail gets steeper, you will need to move your weight backwards to keep your balance. When handling very steep sections, lower your seat and push your body back over the rear wheel. Do not go too fast. On tricky descents, speed is secondary to good technique. As your skills increase, the speed will naturally follow.

Dave Wonderly, one of the best downhill riders in the world, advises,

A diving accident left David Constantine a quadriplegic at the age of 21. Since that time, his life hasn't slowed down much. For his final project at the Royal College of Art in London, he designed and built a device that connects any mountain bike to a wheel-chair. He is shown here using his invention.

ABOVE

Dave Wonderly,
professional rider,
controlling a slide

move. Ride with the **crank arms** parallel to the ground to keep the pedals above the rocks and ruts. It is important to have a good grip on the bar so that unexpected bumps don't tear your hands off (the handlebar)."

The high-speed turns of a descent demand good technique. Wonderly attributes his downhill ability to "knowing how much speed you can take into a corner and still retain traction." He feels it is good to "practice skidding into turns and learning to control the bike when a wheel slides. Feathering the brakes to prevent wheel lock-up reduces the risk of sliding a wheel in a turn."

As your skills progress, you may want to try even trickier maneuvers. **Wheelies**, front and rear wheel hops, and balance can be perfected through practice. A World Trials champion, Hans Rey, suggests, "Get your friends together and make a game out of riding everything you see. Just by attempting difficult moves you'll automatically improve. Set up a neighborhood championship to see who is best in your group."

"Let your arms and legs support your body above the bike as it floats around underneath you absorbing the shocks. Always ride in control and anticipate your next

PREPARATION

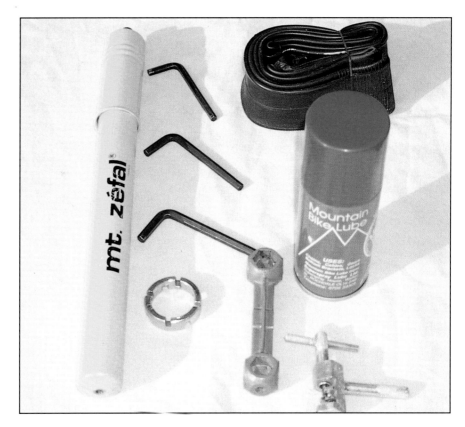

Before every ride, give your bike a quick check to make sure everything is working. If you have **quick release** hubs, check that the skewers are tight. Point the quick release levers to the back of the bike. This will prevent a branch or rock from flipping them open. Quick release hubs make it easier to remove your wheels, and you will not need to carry extra tools to loosen wheel nuts. Make sure your tires are pumped up and the brakes are working properly.

Take a basic tool kit on rides to make sure that you are not left shivering in the rain by a flat tire or mechanical problem. You will need a spare inner tube, **tire levers** to remove the tire from the rim, and a wrench set. A very useful item is a multi-purpose tool that looks like a jack-knife and contains **allen wrenches** and screwdrivers. Many riders carry their tool kits in a small pack under their seats. You will also want to carry a pump with you. This can be attached directly to your bike's frame.

As well as the tools, your kit should include some money for emergencies. Take enough to buy some food if you run out of energy and enough loose change for a phone call. Somewhere in your gear you should also have some sort of identification that gives your name, your address, the name of a person to contact in case of an emergency, and any medical conditions that you might have. Accidents and injuries do happen sometimes, so be prepared. Most importantly, let someone know where you have gone for a ride and when you expect to be back.

Keep an eye on the weather and be prepared for changes in temperature. It is better to take too much clothing than too little. Extra clothes and food can be carried in a pack that straps to your bicycle seat, or in a "fanny pack" — a bag that fits around your waist.

Equip your bike with a cage to hold a water bottle, and take a full bottle on every ride. It is very important to drink a lot of fluids when you are riding. Even when it is cold outside, your body loses a lot of water through activity, and your energy may run low. When the weather is hot, be especially sure to drink liquids before, during, and after a ride, to prevent dehydration.

Deb Murrell warns, "Young and novice riders don't drink enough water.

ABOVE

Practice taking your water bottle out of the cage without looking down.

your eyes off the trail, you could lose control of your bike.

Where can you ride in your area? Your local bike shop should know of trails, and even of groups who go on regular rides. If there are no groups near you, get your friends together and start one. Riding with other bikers brings out the competitive spirit. Do not worry if you fall behind older, more experienced riders. Think of it as a challenge. Every time you ride you will be a little stronger, and soon you will be right up with the best.

When riding with a group, you must stop from time to time to let the slower members catch up. A flat tire or mechanical problem could leave someone stranded on the trail and needing help. Each rider has a responsibility to the rest of the group. Remember that one day it could be you out there alone. Look out for each other.

They just don't realize how serious dehydration can be." She suggests that, "developing a habit of sipping water throughout a ride is very important. Try to finish every ride with an empty bottle."

Practice drinking while riding until you can remove and replace the bottle without looking down. If you take

Cycling fitness comes from riding and having fun on the bike. Each pedal stroke will make you fitter, stronger, and more skillful. Cycling endurance comes from regular training rides over long distances. If you ride for long periods of time and

ride often, you will naturally increase your strength.

See if you are getting faster by timing your favorite ride. Every couple of weeks, ride it as hard as you can. Your time will show how much you have improved.

Do not forget to wear a helmet whenever you ride. Sally Hibberd admits that wearing a helmet, "gives me the confidence to try things I would never dream of without it." While there are no excuses for not wearing one, you will still hear people saying that helmets are uncomfortable or just not cool. When the statistics show that wearing one could save your life, it only makes sense. Hibberd adds, "It becomes so natural to wear it, I forget it's on."

ABOVE and RIGHT

When out with a group, watch out for the other riders. If you are alone, don't take any risks.

COMPETITION

For those who enjoy competition, racing is the best part of mountain biking. Some people race to win, while others just enjoy the atmosphere and the friends they meet. A difficult race can become a competition between you and the course.

Mountain bike races are usually held over two days, with events and categories for all ages and levels of ability. If you are not interested in a strenuous cross-country race, why not test your skills on a trials course or the downhill?

While competing may not be for

everyone, you can learn a lot from going to a race and just watching. Mountain bike courses are great for spectators. Pick a difficult section of the cross-country course and watch how different riders handle the same technical problem. Do they climb in or out of the saddle? What gear are they in and when do they shift? Analyze the line they take through a high speed turn or a rocky descent. You will learn a lot.

The cross-country race is usually the main event for the weekend. The courses combine grueling uphills, rocky descents, and stream crossings. They test the riders' endurance and technical skills to the limit. Although this is the most demanding type of mountain bike competition, it is often the most popular. The races sometimes include up to 300 competitors.

Some courses go just from one

point to another, while others are short and circular. Riders do a different number of laps depending what category they are racing in. Pro races are usually 25 miles (40 kilometers) or longer and can take four hours. The riders must be prepared for mechanical failures, because they cannot accept help or parts from anyone. If they get a flat tire or break a chain, they have to fix it themselves with the tools they carry. They can take food and drink from their teammates, however.

UK mountain bike champion Tim Davies admits that he is addicted to mountain biking. "It's in my system and has become a way of life. I love racing." But he cautions young riders: "Don't sacrifice everything for cycling too soon, especially not your education. A good education should be your first goal. Becoming a good racer is a long process, so be patient.

LEFT

UK champion Tim Davies, one of the growing number of professional riders

RIGHT

Hans Rey, three-time World Trials Champion, at a competition in California

Don't expect to be winning right away. Let your body develop and don't overdo it. Ride to enjoy it."

A trials competition is the ultimate test of a rider's bike-handling skills and concentration.

Boulders, fallen trees, and other natural obstacles are part of a trials course. The competition consists of a number of short technical sections through which the riders must maneuver. Points are taken off the rider's score each time her or his foot touches the ground, or "dabs," with a maximum of five points taken off for falling out of bounds. The rider who has the fewest dabs after everyone has ridden all the sections wins the race.

There are two kinds of trials bikes. Stock trials bikes must have 26-inch (65-cm) wheels and a functional rear

LEFT

One way to get through the traffic

derailleur to qualify for racing. Other bikes fall into the open category, where anything goes. All trials bikes need heavy-duty wheels to withstand the pounding they must endure. The show-offs of the trials race always gather a crowd to witness their gravity-defying hops, twists, and turns over steep cliffs and large boulders.

Hans Rey, who has three times been a world champion trials rider, stresses, "You have to have the basics mastered on the ground before you can perform them three meters (nine feet) up on a boulder. Don't get frustrated by what you see others doing. Start easy, then work up. You can't rush the learning process. It just takes practice—lots of it."

Often races will include either an uphill or downhill time trial, or both. These races are usually against the clock. That is, riders are started individually and ride for the fastest time.

Uphill time trials are usually about 2.5 to 4 miles (4 to 6 km) long. Just because they are short does not mean they are easy. It is a relatively quick race, so there is no holding back. Riders give their all from bottom to top. It takes concentration and determination to block out the pain and just keep going.

On the other hand, a downhill race can be the most action-packed event, with plenty of thrills and spills. Riding at full speed requires total concentration and complete belief in your bike and your own abilities. One small mistake can lead to crashes and sometimes to serious injuries. Usually the best riders wear protective gear. Most are glad they do.

What started as a game between bored competitors waiting for a race award ceremony grew into an organized "hopping" contest. The first hops were over a bent stick that soon evolved into a measuring device called a hopometer. The world record is a hyperhop of over three feet (one meter).

LEAPING LIZARDS

Almost anywhere there are hills to ride, there will be downhill races. Some of the most famous downhill races are in northern California where the mountain bike was born. The Repack in Marin County and the Kamikazee at the Mammoth Mountain ski resort are legendary downhills.

Not to be outdone by their northern neighbors, a group of riders in southern California put on another downhill. What started as a small club race has grown into a world-famous event that draws riders from around the globe. Every year, the Leaping Lizard Freefall brings together an assortment of professional riders and beginners of all ages and backgrounds. Though the individuals are as diverse as the bicycles they bring with them, they share at least one interest. On one weekend each year, they race against the clock, trying to be the next champion of a trail the local riders call Telonix.

My stomach turned with excitement as I rolled my bike to the starting line. In just under 60 seconds, I would be speeding down Telonix. The finish line is about a mile (1.5 km) away and 1,000 feet (300 m) below. Between the top and the

bottom is a combination of fire roads, rutted dirt tracks, weathered sandstone boulders, and muddied hairpin turns. These give the Leaping Lizard Freefall the reputation for being one of the most radical downhill races anywhere.

Almost fifty speed-merchants waited restlessly with me for their turn to hurl themselves downward. Some of the best bike handlers in the world were among them. Looking around me, the lack of flashy lycra clothing was apparent.

Dave Wonderly,
the eventual
winner, about to
catch some big air
off a jump on the
second day of
racing

Serious riders judge each other not by what they wear, but how they perform on the threshold of complete adrenalin overload. Each year the times get faster as the maniacs push their personal limits.

Most have practiced the course until every rock, turn, and bump is memorized. If they have any time-saving techniques, they keep it to themselves.

"Ten seconds."

I sucked down deep breaths and focused my eyes on the sandstone under the front tire. The timer counted off the last few seconds of sanity.

"5, 4, 3, 2, 1, Go!"

The Leaping Lizard Freefall had begun. In seconds I was pedaling hard and fast over the crest of the hill. The wind roared past my ears and brought tears to my eyes. The cactus and sagebrush lining the course became a blur as I passed the point of no return (or the point of no stopping, anyway). Steering the bike through the rocky twists and turns, I feathered the brakes only enough to stay in

control. At this speed even a small mistake would send me flying off the trail and into a cactus. Spectators were gathered near the large boulder section with the hope of watching the riders **catch air** off the natural jumps. A rough section near the finish almost tore my hands off the handlebar. I gripped it even tighter than before.

Leg muscles burning and arms numb, I roared past the finish line two minutes and twenty seconds later. Race over, pressure off, I hiked back up the trail to watch those who were following me down. One by one, the downhillers flew past on their way to the finish below.

The fastest time of the day was

turned in by Dave Wonderly with a mind-numbing one minute fifty seconds. This new course record beat his previous best by nine seconds and once again proved that he is truly the champion of Telonix. My two minutes and twenty seconds seemed a little bit slow in comparison, but at least I got down (some people didn't), and I had some serious fun, too.

Racing is not for everyone. It is about pushing yourself to the limits of personal performance. Dedication is needed to endure the painful excitement competition delivers. No flashy clothing or expensive bike will make you go fast without training, practice, and an unwavering belief in yourself.

Tim Gould, one of the most talented riders in the sport, advises racers to "set realistic goals. Start with local events and go from there. It's a long, gradual climb to the top so don't expect to compete at championship levels too soon. Don't get discouraged, and have fun."

Those who finish a difficult race

BELOW

Races also go uphill. They're not as fast, but they're even harder work!

have the reward of knowing they did their best. Even if you come in last, you will have learned something about your cycling and will be stronger for having experienced it. You will also have met many new friends.

"Keep things in perspective," says three-time world champion Sara Ballantine. "See how you're improving race to race, rather than comparing yourself with the best in the world. Let your abilities develop naturally."

MAINTENANCE

Proper care and maintenance of your bike will increase its life and give you a lot more hassle-free rides. Mountain bikes get exposed to mud, water, and heavy abuse, so they need care and attention if you want them to work properly. Regular maintenance will keep your bike functioning like new and ensure a safe ride. Speeding downhill is not the time to wonder if you should have replaced those frayed brake cables.

The mountain bike has a lot of pivoting parts, sliding cables, and rolling bearings that depend on proper cleaning, lubrication, and adjustment. Although bikes operate on a simple concept, maintaining one requires special tools and a gentle touch. Bike maintenance skills, like riding techniques, develop slowly through patience and practice.

Begin by learning what the components do and how they feel and sound when you are riding. Learn about the functions of the derailleurs, brakes, and wheels. Knowing how they work is vital to understanding how to care for your bicycle properly.

The best maintenance is the preventive kind, in which you try to

Computers are becoming a vital tool to the designers of mountain bikes and bike components. Computer programs can test new designs before the bike is built, which saves both time and money.

locate and correct problems before they cause damage. Keeping your bike clean and lubricated is the simplest and most important form of preventive maintenance. Keeping the grease and grime off the moving parts reduces wear, and a clean bike is easier to adjust.

A bucket of soapy water and a brush will take care of wheels, tires, and the crankset. A soapy cloth or sponge should be used on paint, and an old toothbrush works wonders on

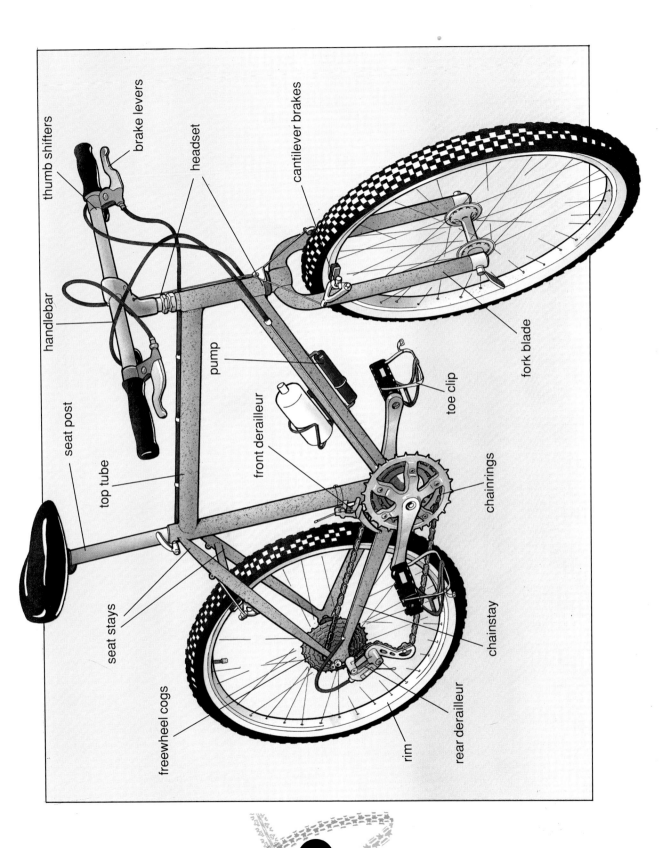

thumb shifters

brake levers

cantilever brakes

headset

handlebar

seat post

top tube

pump

front derailleur

toe clip

fork blade

seat stays

chainrings

chainstay

freewheel cogs

rim

rear derailleur

RIGHT

Keep your bike
clean and it will
last longer.

small parts. Commercial solvents will clean the chain and derailleurs.

When you are rinsing your bike, be careful to avoid spraying water around the **bottom bracket, headset,** and hubs. This forces in dirt and water and leads to damage of the bearings. Ask experienced riders how they clean their bikes.

While cleaning your bike, check for damage and potential problems. Look out for frayed cables, loose or worn parts, and cracks or wrinkles in the paint that could indicate a bent or broken frame or fork blade. Spin the wheels. If the rims rub irregularly against the brake pads, they may be bent, or out of **true.** If something is loose or out of adjustment, take it to a bicycle shop for repair. Ignoring problems can lead to further damage. Every time you ride, you also trust your own safety to the quality of maintenance the bike has received. So make a point of keeping it in good shape.

Lubrication is vital. It keeps the moving parts sliding and rolling smoothly. Different parts of your bike need different kinds of lubricants. Chains and derailleurs receive light oils, and bearings use thicker grease. Many different types of lubrication exist so it is easy to get confused. Ask your bike shop sales people what they recommend.

In addition to keeping your bike clean and lubricated, you must make sure it is properly adjusted. Each part needs special attention. Parts that are either too loose or too tight can cause damage. It takes practice and attention to develop the delicate feel required for proper maintenance. It is a good idea to watch more experienced riders or mechanics working on bikes. You will learn a lot by asking them questions. Bike manuals are also a good learning source. Look for them at your bookstore or library.

Tim Davies advises, "I make sure everything is adjusted and tight before I leave home on a ride. This cuts down problems out on the trail and cuts down on the amount of tools I have to carry."

BELOW

Before you go out, check the bike over and make sure everything is working.

LAND ACCESS

A s mountain biking grows, so do the problems of land access. Just because you have the ability to go almost anywhere on your bike does not mean you have the right to do so. Vast areas of public and private land are being closed to mountain bikers both in the United States and Europe at an alarming rate. Open, undeveloped land is one of the world's most precious natural resources.

As land development and population grow, outdoor enthusiasts have less and less room. The demand for access to public land is growing as the amount of land decreases.

The future does not promise easy solutions to this scarcity of land. People will continue to leave behind their busy lives in cities to search for peace and serenity in the country and on mountain trails.

As mountain bikes make it easier for more people to enjoy the great outdoors, cyclists are using many areas used by both hikers and horseback riders. Some established users view mountain bikers as unwanted invaders of their favorite spots. In many cases, this conflict has led to land closures for mountain bikes. Many of these problems were caused by a few unthinking people who gave all mountain bikers a bad name. Every rider has to act in such a way that further closures are prevented.

Y̊ou will be sharing the trails with many different users, so be on the lookout. When you meet hikers or people on horseback, give them the right of way. Do not skid or yell to get their attention. They are there for the peace and quiet. When

The strong frame and wheels, good brakes, and multiple gears of the mountain bike make it a good bike for touring. From a long day trip to a transcontinental ride, cyclists are continually exploring the less-traveled places of our world. Special packs called panniers can be used to carry clothing and gear.

RIGHT

Be careful of others on the trail such as horseback riders. They have a right to be there too.

approaching others, be prepared to slow down and to stop if necessary to let them pass. Be especially careful when dealing with horses. Give them plenty of room and make no sudden movements.

Some people will get out of your way, but do not expect it. Be sure to thank them if they do. Above all, be friendly. Just because some hikers interrupted your favorite descent does not give you the right to be angry at them. They are allowed to be there too. Other people are not enemies. They are your partners

in using and caring for the land.

During your off-road travel, you will encounter people who do not like mountain biking and may tell you so. It is not worth arguing with these people. It is best just to say, "I'm sorry you feel that way," and keep riding.

Respect closed areas. If you are in doubt, get permission. Sneaking onto illegal trails will only damage mountain biking's image. There will be times when your favorite trail is too crowded to enjoy. Look for another time or place to ride. A Sunday afternoon on a local horse trail may not be the best time for a hard training ride. If you need the speed,

RIGHT and BELOW

Because of damage to the land, large areas in Europe and the United States are being closed to riders.

investigate the local race scene, or start a race of your own.

As well as dealing with other users, you must be aware of how the mountain bike can affect the environment. While tearing a new path cross-country is hard to resist, this sort of riding severely damages vegetation and topsoil. This leads to erosion. It takes years for nature to heal just a moment of thoughtlessness. Stay on the established trails and leave untracked meadows and steep hillsides for viewing, not riding.

Try not to lock up your wheels just to skid for fun. Tire tracks can create channels for water and cause erosion. Test your handling skills by controlling your speed without locking up. **Switchback turns** are designed to channel water away from the trail, and cutting the corners can lead to irreparable damage. While burying your bike up to the axles on a muddy trail may be fun, think about the damage you are causing to the trail.

Pack out what you have packed in. Leaving no trace of your presence should be your goal. By developing an attitude and cycling skills that reduce the bicycle's impact on the environment, you will help keep mountain biking areas open.

BELOW

Would you want to ride through wasteland like this? If not, it is in your interest to cooperate with other land users and try to prevent erosion.

Glossary

Allen wrench A six-sided tool used to adjust many components on a mountain bike. The most common sizes are 4, 5, and 6 mm.

Bottom bracket The assembly that connects the crankset to the frame

Cadence Pedaling rhythm

Catch air To momentarily ride with both wheels off the ground when your bike hits a natural rise or dip in the trail

Chainrings The rings of the crankset that the chain rides on

Coaster brakes A type of bicycle brake that is applied by pedaling backwards

Crank arms The parts of a bicycle that connect the pedals to the bottom bracket

Crankset The assembly to which the pedals and bottom bracket are connected

Derailleurs The mechanisms that shift a bicycle's gears by moving the chain up and down on the chainrings or on the freewheel cogs connected to the rear wheel

Feathering A method of braking in which the front and rear levers are gently squeezed and released to control speed and prevent wheel skid

Freewheel The assembly that supports the cogs on the rear wheel. It also lets the wheel turn without the pedals going around.

Headset The set of bearings located at either end of the head tube. The headset connects the fork to the frame.

Quick release A device using a lever and skewer, instead of a nut and bolt, for easy removal or adjustment of wheels and seat posts

Slalom A race on a zigzag course where riders go through gates

Switchback turn A very tight turn that leads back in almost the direction the road came from

Tire lever A tool used to remove a bicycle tire from the rim of the wheel

True In line. Used to describe a wheel without bumps or bends in the rim

Wheelie Riding technique in which the front wheel is pulled off the ground

More Information

American Bicycle Association (ABA)
P.O. Box 718
Chandler, Arizona 85244 USA

National Bicycle League (NBL)
P.O. Box 729
Dublin, Ohio 43017 USA

United States Cycling Federation (USCF)
1750 E. Boulder
Colorado Springs, Colorado 80909 USA

Books

Abramowski, Dwain. *Mountain Bikes.* New York, New York: Franklin Watts, 1990.

Ballantine, Richard. *Richard's New Bicycle Book.* New York, New York: Ballantine Books, 1987.

Coello, Dennis L. *The Complete Mountain Biker.* New York, New York: Lyons & Burford, 1989.

Strassman, Michael A. *The Basic Essentials of Mountain Biking.* Merrillville, Indiana: ICS Books, Inc., 1989.

Van der Plas, Rob. *The Mountain Bike Book.* San Francisco, California: Bicycle Books, 1990.

Index